TOM HUDDLESTON

A long time ago in a galaxy
far, far away . . . .

ADVENTURES IN

WILD SPACE

T H E   D A R K

It is a time of darkness. With the end of the Clone Wars and the destruction of the Jedi Order, the evil Emperor Palpatine rules the galaxy unopposed.

After their parents were kidnapped by

CHAPTER 1

INMATES

If he stood right up on his tiptoes, Milo Graf was just able to peer out through the porthole set high into the wall of their cramped cell. Through it he could see nothing but a blanket of deep green, dotted with flecks of white. In the centre was a tiny black smudge, getting smaller and smaller as the star freighter *Moveable Feast* rose into the upper atmosphere.

That shrinking dot was Capital City, bustling hub of the planet Lothal – and they were leaving it behind. Leaving behind their ship the *Whisper Bird*, stuck on an old landing strip, in need of repairs. Leaving behind Milo's beloved Kowakian monkey-lizard Morq, who hadn't spent a day without his master since he hatched from his egg.

And leaving behind their new friends Mira and Ephraim Bridger, who had helped Milo and his sister Lina right when they needed it most. The Bridgers had been the only ones who might have been able to help the Graf children find their parents – so they were leaving that hope behind, too.

'We'll see them again,' Lina said, putting her arms protectively around her brother. 'I know we will.'

'No, you don't,' Milo said softly. He could see the curve of the planet now, where the emerald shimmer of Lothal gave way to the blackness of space. 'But thanks for trying to make me feel better.'

He turned, putting on his best smile. Lina ruffled his hair.

'What we need is some kind of plan,' she said. 'There has to be a way out of here. A freighter like this wasn't designed to hold prisoners; the Shade must have converted one of the cargo bays. So maybe there's something she missed.'

She turned, inspecting the narrow cell. Three of the walls were plate durasteel, interrupted only by the little porthole. The fourth was a lattice of bars each as thick as Milo's arm, inset with a sturdy gate and secured by a bulky electronic lock. It looked out into a broad hallway lined with more cells, three on either side.

Lina peered out. 'There's a control panel down there, by that door,' she said. 'Maybe we could throw something, try to hit it. Take off one of your shoes.'

'Why my shoes?' Milo asked. 'Why not one of yours?'

'OK, one of mine,' Lina said, reaching down. 'If we hit the panel square on, maybe it'll trigger the lock.'

Milo looked doubtful. 'Captain Mondatha... I mean the Shade, she may be evil but she's not stupid. I don't think she'd put the cell controls right where anyone could get to them.'

'Well, it's worth a try,' Lina said, leaning out through the bars and taking aim. 'Maybe she doesn't expect us to try a trick like this, 'cos we're just kids. Or maybe she really is that dumb.'

'You'll find I'm not.' A woman's voice echoed through the empty corridor. Milo recognised the icy tones of the bounty hunter who had betrayed and imprisoned them back on Lothal. 'Throw, if you want to sit here in the dark. That's a light switch.'

Shalla Mondatha – or the Shade, as she preferred to be known – had been set on their trail by Captain Korda, the Imperial officer who had taken their parents. Now he was after the Graf children too, desperate to get his hands on their droid, CR-8R, and the maps he was carrying around in his cranial databanks. Maps to Wild Space, and the many worlds that the Grafs had spent their lives exploring. What he'd do with the maps when he found them only Korda knew for sure, but Milo and Lina were determined not to let him have them.

'Where are you taking us?' Lina demanded, not sure where to direct her angry stare.

'To Korda, of course,' the voice came back. 'I just have one small errand, then I'll let him know where to pick you up. The droid, too.'

'Where's CR-8R?' Milo demanded. 'What have you done with him?'

'Oh, he's unharmed,' the Shade told him. 'Look.'

The heavy door at the end of the cell block slid open and a familiar figure floated in. CR-8R drifted towards them, hovering on his repulsors. His golden eyes lit up when he saw the children.

'Oh, Mistress Lina, Master Milo,' the droid fussed. 'I'm so pleased to see you both safe and –'

'Quiet,' the Shade snapped. CR-8R's voice stopped dead. 'You see? I can make him do whatever I want.'

Lina reached out, taking CR-8R's hand. 'A restraining bolt,' she said, seeing the sturdy metal stud locked onto the droid's breastplate. 'Oh, Crater. I'm so sorry.'

CR-8R stared back helplessly, and Milo knew that as long as that bolt was in place the droid would be unable to help them.

'As you see, all three of you are under my control,' the Shade cut in. 'Behave yourselves, and it will all be over soon.'

'Let us go!' Lina shouted out, her temper fraying. 'You'll pay for this, I swear.'

'No, no,' the Shade said coldly. 'I'll get paid for this. Very different.' Through the speakers they heard the drone of an alarm. 'Good. They're here.'

The speakers cut out. Lina shook her head bitterly.

'Don't blame yourself, Mistress Lina,' CR-8R said. 'If it's any consolation, I was fooled too. She did seem very friendly.'

'Well, that's the last time we trust a stranger,' Lina sighed. 'Come here, let me take a look at that bolt.'

Milo turned back to the porthole. Lothal was distant now, a hazy green disc on a blanket of shimmering stars.

Then with a start he noticed that one

of the stars was moving. There was a ship out there, catching the light from Lothal's sun as it banked towards them.

'Someone's coming,' he told his sister.

Lina joined him at the window. The speck of light was now recognisably a craft, its boxy, grey-white body framed by short, downward-facing wings. Laser cannons swivelled on either side of the sloping cockpit.

'An Imperial troop transport,' Lina observed.

The craft dipped its wings as it circled above the *Moveable Feast*. Milo saw docking clamps extending from the base.

'Is it Korda?' he asked, feeling the pit of his stomach plummet. 'Has he come for us?'

There was a thud as the transport docked. The cell walls shook.

'I don't know,' Lina said. 'And I don't want to find out. Crater, come here. If I

can prise that bolt off maybe we've got a chance.'

She reached through the bars, grasping at the collar around CR-8R's neck. She pulled as hard as she could, clawing with her nails. Milo heard a snap and there was a flash of light.

Lina leapt back. 'Yowch!' she said. 'That hurt.'

'I'm afraid the restraining bolt has

been fitted with an electric charge to prevent tampering,' CR-8R explained.

'Why didn't you tell me before?' Lina asked furiously.

'Captain Mondatha ordered me not to,' CR-8R said. 'She thought it would be funny.'

'And it was.' The Shade strode through the open doorway, shooting them a thin, humourless smile. She wore a dark green robe that flapped at her ankles and her boot heels rang on the metal floor. 'Honestly girl, what kind of fool do you take me for?'

'The kind that locks up kids and makes deals with the Empire,' Lina shot back. 'Korda will kill you just for having seen us.'

'He might try,' the bounty hunter admitted. 'He wouldn't be the first. But that's later. Now, join me in welcoming our guests.'

Milo felt his heartbeat quicken as a pair of Imperial stormtroopers marched in lockstep through the doorway. Their armour gleamed, helmets turning left and right as their black eyes scanned the cell block.

'You said you weren't taking us to him right away,' Milo protested. 'You said –'

'Be quiet,' the Shade snapped. 'They're dropping off, not picking up. Not everything is about you.'

As she spoke, Milo noticed that each of the troopers had a length of metal chain wrapped around his fist. One gave a tug and an alien stumbled through the doorway, almost tripping as he lurched into the cell block. He was a Lasat, Milo quickly identified, a large humanoid species from the Outer Rim planet Lasan, with a barrel chest and bulging arms. He raised his bald head and Milo saw that his face was looped with scars, from tiny pockmarks to great grooves cut deep into his skin. His eyes were cast into shadow by his shelf-like forehead.

A human male followed, bound like the first by the wrists and ankles. He was the complete opposite of his fellow prisoner, pale and skinny with a shock of red hair standing upright on his bobbing head. The young man shot Milo

a friendly wink, his green eyes gleaming.

The troopers nodded a greeting to Captain Mondatha. 'Payment on arrival at Noctu, as agreed,' said one.

'Provided they're still in one piece,' the other put in.

'They won't give me any trouble,' the Shade assured them, gesturing to a large cell at the far end of the corridor. 'You can put the big one down there. The other can go in here.'

One of the troopers shoved the red-haired man into the cell opposite Milo and Lina, slamming the gate behind him. The Shade tapped in a code and the lock slid home.

'Hey, what are those two in for?' the prisoner asked, gesturing at the Graf children.

The Shade frowned. 'I'm teaching them what happens if you don't eat your vegetables.'

The Lasat lumbered along the corridor, barely glancing at Milo and Lina as he passed. The trooper yanked the chain impatiently and the prisoner stumbled, letting out a grunt.

'I told you what'd happen if you did that again,' the scarred alien said, his voice a grinding rumble like stones in an avalanche.

'Quiet, scum,' the trooper said, giving the chain another tug.

The Lasat staggered again. But instead of falling he lunged at the trooper, shoving him forward. The trooper hit the cell gate with a crunch and rebounded into the massive prisoner, who wrapped his arms around the trooper's chest and began to squeeze.

The second stormtrooper shoved past the Shade, grabbing the big alien and trying to pull him away. But the prisoner swept out with one massive arm, knocking the trooper off his feet. Milo and Lina jerked back as the trooper slammed into the bars of their cell and fell in a clattering heap to the floor.

The Shade took a step forward, drawing something from her belt – a durasteel pole about as long as her arm. She flicked a switch and blue energy rippled along the shaft.

She tapped the convict lightly on the back of the neck with the tip of the pole. There was a spark and the Lasat slumped, unconscious before he hit the floor.

The trooper fought free from beneath the big alien's body, rolling and shoving the sleeping giant into his cell and slamming the door.

The Shade tapped in the lock code. 'Seemed like you needed help,' she said. 'Don't worry, it won't cost you extra.'

'We could've handled it,' the trooper grunted. His companion was picking himself up, brushing the dust from his armour.

'Of course you could,' the bounty hunter agreed politely. 'Now please, allow me to escort you back to your ship. Droid, with me.'

As the door slid shut behind them, Milo heard a strange wheezing noise. The younger prisoner was sitting on the floor of the opposite cell, rocking back and forth with tears of laughter streaming down his face.

'Did you see that?' he asked, slapping his leg. 'Beautiful. Just beautiful. That Davin, he's not exactly a charmer but he does have his moments.'

Milo looked at the prone figure lying in the next cell. The alien's chest rose and fell, snores echoing from the steel walls.

'So, what are you in for, really?' the red-haired convict asked when his laughter had subsided.

Lina eyed him suspiciously. 'That's our business,' she said.

The man held up his hands. 'Sure it is,' he said. 'You're a little younger than I'd expect is all. But I'm sure the Empire have their reasons. They always do, right?' He winked again.

'Did that trooper say we're going to Noctu?' Milo asked.

The man nodded. 'Sure are,' he said. 'Straight to the asteroid mines. And you know no-one ever comes back from there… Still, it's my own fault. I shouldn't have gotten caught. I talk too much, that's my trouble.'

He shook his head ruefully. 'Name's Stel, by the way. And that lump of meat over there, that's Davin. But you don't really need to know that, because he won't speak to you, and if you've got any sense you won't speak to him neither.'

'He's... dangerous?' Milo asked.

Stel laughed. 'Dangerous? Davin?' he snorted. 'You never heard of the butcher of Brentaal IV?'

Milo shook his head.

'They only caught him last week,' Stel said. 'He's been on the run for years, outwitting them at every turn. But they ran him down in the end. But look, don't mention any of this stuff when he wakes up, OK? He's a little touchy, in case you didn't notice.'

Milo shook his head quickly, watching as the pale man lay back, resting his head against the wall and closing his eyes.

'He seems friendly,' he whispered to Lina. 'Maybe –'

'Don't say it,' Lina said quickly. 'This time, we're going to figure things out on our own.'

CHAPTER 2

ADRIFT

'Does he ever shut up?' Milo whispered as Stel's voice droned through the prison block.

'Well, sometimes he's asleep,' Lina reminded him.

She had to admit, her brother had a point. She didn't know how long it had been since the two prisoners had been brought in, but Stel had been talking for most of it.

They'd heard the Imperial craft detach, and shortly afterwards Lina had felt that familiar rolling lurch in her stomach and knew the *Moveable Feast* had made the jump to hyperspace. Stel had dropped off to sleep and soon the children had done the same, curling up together on the hard metal floor. Lina had awoken to find Milo clutching her arm so tightly it was almost painful, muttering and twitching in his sleep. For a moment she thought they were back on the *Whisper Bird*, in the little cot they'd sometimes shared on long space voyages, back when they were small.

But when she sat up and opened her eyes, it had all come flooding back. This cramped cell, those sturdy bars, that piercing light. And worst of all a pair of eyes staring at her, unflinching and hard. Davin squatted on his haunches, his fists clenched. Lina had tried giving him a friendly wave, but the Lasat had just hung his head.

Stel had awoken shortly afterwards, and after greeting his fellow inmates with a cheery grin he'd started talking and, so far, he'd forgotten to stop. He'd told them about his childhood on Lothal, how he'd grown up in his uncle's repair shop and learned everything there was to know about ships, before going on to the Academy where he learned everything there was to know about the Republic and the Empire and every other subject under the sun.

'You need the answer to any question, big or small, you just ask old Stel,' he was saying. 'Exobiology, engine maintenance, the best drinking den in Mos Eisley spaceport – you name it, just ask.'

'How do we get out of here?' Lina asked, only half joking.

Stel looked at her, and for a brief moment he was silent. Then he slapped his leg and laughed. 'You got me, sister,' he said. 'That one, I do not know.'

'Also, when's she going to feed us?'

Milo wondered.

Again, Stel looked stumped. 'That's a good one, too,' he admitted. 'It's been hours, right? And nothing but a cup of cold water.' He drained the small tin cup, tossing it aside with a clang. 'That droid said he'd come back right away, and he never did. Here, take this for now.'

He threw something through the bars into Milo's lap. It was a food bar, Imperial issue.

'Where did you get that?' Lina wondered suspiciously.

'One of those stormtrooper boys on the last ship,' Stel said. 'I can be pretty charming when I want to be.'

'Aren't you hungry?' Milo asked him.

'Sure,' Stel shrugged. 'But I can wait. I know growing boys need to eat.'

'Thank you,' Lina said as Milo tore the bar open and began to chew. 'You're very kind.'

She almost gave the young man a friendly smile, then she stopped herself. They could trust no-one. However nice they might seem.

She thought back to CR-8R's last appearance. It was as Stel had said: the droid had handed each of them a tin cup filled with stale, ship-stored water, and Milo had asked when they were going to eat. CR-8R had promised to return as soon as he'd served his mistress, but he never came back.

Lina felt a twinge of discomfort. CR-8R would never let them down, he'd know they must be starving by now. But he didn't have control over his own body. Maybe he wanted to come back, but the Shade wouldn't allow it.

'So what's the deal with this bounty hunter?' Stel asked, pressing his face between the bars. 'You known her long?'

'Not long,' Milo said. 'She seemed nice

at first, then she turned on us.'

Lina shot him a stern glance, warning him not to say any more.

'That's how these mercenary types work,' Stel agreed. 'They seem friendly, then blammo. You're locked away for something you didn't even do. This one time –'

There was a rumbling thud from somewhere deep inside the ship and the lights in the ceiling flickered. Stel broke off, looking around uncertainly. Davin was sitting upright, his eyes glinting.

The sound came again and suddenly they were plunged into complete blackness. Lina pushed Milo behind her, facing the corridor. But the dark only lasted a few moments before the lights buzzed and flickered back on, a little dimmer than before.

'What just happened?' Milo asked.

'We're out of hyperspace,' Stel

told them.

The ship rocked beneath them and Lina almost lost her balance, reaching out to grip the bars. 'We're adrift,' she said, her feeling of unease deepening. Where was CR-8R?

She was distracted by a deafening slam from outside the cell. Davin was standing upright, his cup clutched in his hand. As Lina watched he drove it into the bars with all his might. The steel gate shook but stayed firm. The tin cup crumpled but Davin punched again, driving his fist into the bars, using the cup as a shield. The noise of metal on metal resounded from the prison walls.

'Well, at least someone's got a plan,' Stel said, but Lina could hear the discomfort in his voice. They had enough to worry about without that monster getting loose.

'Attention prisoner!' a shrill voice

barked, and an eerie blue light filled the
cell block. 'Any attempt to escape will be
met with retaliatory force!'

The air outside Davin's cell
shimmered and a figure appeared. It
was the Shade – or at least a hologram
of her, projected from a tiny glass eye
set into the floor. The form was outlined
in blue, one hand raised. But the image

was fuzzy, rippling and breaking like a reflection in choppy water.

Davin shook his head, and slammed his fist into the bars again.

'You have been warned!' the hologram barked. Then a bolt of energy shot from the projector housing, missing Davin by centimetres. It hit the wall and rebounded back into the hologram, which fizzled and disappeared. The alien kept pounding away.

'Great security system,' Stel said sarcastically. 'Really, super effective.'

'It seems like the whole ship's on the blink,' Lina said. 'The lights, the engines. But where's the Shade?'

'Maybe she's trying to fix it,' Milo suggested.

'Or maybe she's out of action,' Stel offered darkly. 'Maybe something happened to her. Maybe she got sick. Maybe we're stuck on a drifting ship light

years from anywhere, and all they'll find
in a hundred years is four little skeletons
still locked in these curse-it cells!' And he
slammed the bars in frustration.

'Don't talk like that,' Lina said. 'It
isn't helpful. And besides, we do have a
chance. If all the systems are out, maybe
that means...'

'Crater!' Milo cried, and Lina turned
to see the cell-block door sliding open
and a familiar shape floating through.

'Crater!' she cried. 'You're OK!'

The droid drifted towards them,
clapping one hand to his metal forehead
in relief. 'And so are you both,' he said.
'The whole time I was stuck in there, I
was terrified for your safety.'

'Stuck in where, Crater?' Milo asked.
'What's going on?'

'I'm not sure,' the droid admitted.
'After I brought the Captain her lunch,
she ordered me to seal myself in a storage

closet and stay there until she called for me. I tried to protest, Master Milo, honestly I did. I know how bad-tempered you get when you're hungry.'

Stel barked a laugh and Milo blushed.

'But I had no choice,' CR-8R insisted. 'Anyway, after some time I saw the lights go out and felt the ship start to drift. I realised the restraining bolt was no longer operating. I left the closet, but there was no sign of Captain Mondatha. I decided I should check on you first before I looked into the source of the problem. Besides, it's very dark out there.'

'You did good, Crater,' Lina said. 'Now can you get us out of here?'

'Right away,' CR-8R said and tapped the code into the keypad. The gate swung open.

'I can honestly say I have never been more pleased to see a droid in my life,'

Stel grinned through the bars of his cell. 'Now get me out of here and we can go see what's happened to the ship.'

CR-8R looked at Lina, who bit her lip. Then slowly she shook her head. 'I'm sorry,' she said. 'But we don't know you. We'll let you know what's going on as soon as we figure it out.'

Stel's face dropped. 'You're leaving me

here? With that?'

He jerked a thumb at Davin, who had stopped hammering and was watching them all keenly.

'You shouldn't go out there,' he said suddenly, his eyes fixed on Lina.

She looked at the Lasat in surprise. Was that supposed to be a caution, or a threat? Did Davin know more than he was letting on? But the giant just stared back, his grey eyes shadowed by his jutting brow.

Lina broke away, turning back to Stel. 'I'm really sorry,' she said. 'We've had some bad experiences with strangers lately.' Milo was already waiting in the doorway. Behind him all was darkness.

'I gave you a food bar!' Stel protested. 'I told you my whole life story, I thought we were friends!'

'I'm sure we will be,' Lina said apologetically, joining her brother.

'When this is all over, I'll make it up to you. I promise. Just sit tight.'

'No!' Stel cried desperately before the door slid shut, cutting him off. The darkness deepened and Lina let out a long breath. The air in the corridor was still and cold.

'We'll come back for him, won't we?' Milo asked.

'Sure we will,' Lina said. 'But first let's get up to the bridge.'

Behind them she heard a slam, and another, and another. Davin, she thought. I really hope those bars are as solid as they look.

CHAPTER 3

IN THE DARK

'Switch on your beams, Crater,' Milo suggested as they followed the droid into the deepening darkness. A dull gleam leaked from beneath CR-8R's cranial dome and a series of blinking red lights marked the edges of the walkway. But otherwise the corridor was pitch black.

'I'm afraid my power is running very low,' the droid told him. 'I haven't had the chance to recharge since we were on the *Whisper Bird*. We have no idea how much power is in the ship's cells, or how long this situation will take to resolve. I'd hate to shut down just when you needed me most.'

'You're right, Crater,' Lina agreed. 'Besides, a little darkness never hurt anyone. Right?'

'I guess,' Milo said uncertainly. He'd never been afraid of the dark, exactly. But he'd never been fond of it either.

'I can see perfectly clearly with my infrared,' CR-8R said. 'I will guide you.'

There was a sudden metallic clang and Lina let out a yell. CR-8R's head swivelled round.

'I'm OK,' Lina said through gritted teeth. 'I just walked into something pointy. Thanks for the warning, Crater. We can't all float, remember?"

The droid peered down. 'It appears to be a toolbox of some kind,' he said. 'My apologies, Mistress Lina. I shall endeavour to be more observant in future.'

The droid led them on, and Milo

realised his eyes were beginning to adjust. Ahead of them rose a steep flight of steps.

'These stairs lead to the cargo bay,' CR-8R explained. 'On the other side of that is the bridge.'

'And that's where we'll get our answers,' Lina said.

As Milo climbed, he tried to build a mental picture of the *Moveable Feast*, from what he'd seen in the docking bay back on Lothal. It was a large ship – not as bulky as an Imperial freighter, but a lot bigger than the *Whisper Bird*. He remembered the body of the craft rising above him and he'd seen the cockpit too, or at least a row of windows on the front of the craft.

There was a metallic creak and the ship tilted sickeningly. Milo staggered into the railing, lurching out into empty space. Lina grabbed hold, pulling him back.

'The artificial gravity's weakening,' she said as the tilting stopped and the *Moveable Feast* settled back into position.

'What could do this?' Milo asked. 'Fry all the ship's systems at once?'

'I don't know,' Lina admitted. 'Some kind of computer virus? A bug in the system? I won't know until we reach the bridge.'

'Here's the door,' CR-8R said, tapping in a code. 'Be careful now. Just follow the sound of my –'

'Not do move!' a voice shrieked, and a pale-blue hologram flickered into life in front of them. The Shade stood in the doorway, her arms crossed. 'Go back cell immedi-edi-edi. You been have warneded!'

CR-8R paused, staring the hologram in the face. 'Oh, do be quiet,' he muttered, and drifted through the doorway. His metal skin shone blue as he broke through the hologram and out the other side.

'Stop!' the hologram shrieked. 'Stop right! Steps will be take-ake-ake!'

Milo looked up at the stern, flickering figure. There was something creepy about the hologram shimmering like a spectre in the darkness, its recorded message glitching and repeating.

'Go on, Lo-Bro,' Lina gave him a gentle push from behind. 'It's not going to hurt you.'

Milo took a step through, and the hologram turned with him. 'Cease!' it bellowed. 'You been have warned-ed-ed-ed-ed-ed!'

The figure twitched manically as if it was being electrocuted, screaming the same syllable over and over. The shrill voice echoed back from the walls and the ceiling like an alarm. 'Dead! Dead! Dead!' it seemed to cry, the sounds clashing and blurring until Milo was forced to cover his ears.

Lina pushed through, gritting her teeth. In the silver-edged light Milo could see out into the cargo bay, towering stacks of crates rising towards a shadowy ceiling.

Then the door slid shut and the hologram vanished abruptly, plunging them into darkness.

'Well that was incredibly creepy,' Lina said, and Milo stifled a laugh.

Now the darkness was absolute. He waved a hand in front of his face but could see nothing, even when he accidentally slapped himself on the nose.

'Just follow my voice,' CR-8R called out. 'It isn't far.'

Milo stuck out his arms, feeling his way cautiously. The floor underfoot was solid steel but the walls were uneven, just piles of stacked boxes and containers.

'What's in all these crates, Crater?' he asked as they made their way deeper into the darkness.

'Captain Mondatha told me not to ask,' the droid told him. 'I suspect that whatever it is, it's not entirely legal.'

'Sansanna spice?' Lina asked.

'I don't think so,' CR-8R admitted. 'We would be able to smell it. This was something else. I saw a word printed on several of the containers. Cylo.' He spelled it out for them.

'Means nothing to me,' Lina admitted.

'There's a sharp turn here,' CR-8R warned them. 'So be- oh!'

Milo froze. 'Crater? Are you OK?'

'Quite alright,' the droid said. 'I just... Never mind.'

'What is it, Crater?' Lina asked. 'If

you've seen something weird, you should tell us. I know you don't want us to be scared, but it's better if we know exactly what's going on.'

'It really isn't important,' CR-8R insisted. 'I just brushed into something, that's all.'

'What about your infrared?' Milo asked.

'It didn't show up on my infrared,' the droid admitted as Milo and Lina came up behind him. 'It seems to be a membrane of some sort. It's so fine, it was almost invisible.'

Milo reached out. At first he could feel nothing, then his hand brushed against something soft and ever-so-slightly sticky. It wrapped around his fingers and he pulled back, the substance vibrating as he did so.

'Hang on, didn't you come this way a few moments ago?' Lina asked. 'On your way to the cell block?'

'It wasn't here then,' CR-8R said. 'That's why I was surprised. But I'm sure it's nothing. Let's just keep moving. Maybe just a little faster.'

The droid drifted on, his repulsors humming. Milo followed, alert to every creak and groan of the ship around them.

After a few moments the echo of their footsteps changed and Milo knew they had entered a more open space. There was a brief flash of white light and he saw that they were standing in the centre of a wide circle of crates.

And as the light faded he thought he saw something else too – a tiny shape, low to the ground. It was moving.

'That light came from underneath us,' Lina said, looking down.

The flash came again, a jagged electric spark, and Milo saw that she was right. There appeared to be a hole in the floor, off to their left. It was roughly circular, about two arm-spans wide and ragged around the edges, as though something had melted or chewed through the durasteel deck.

Lina and Milo stood on the edge, peering down. The light came again, sparks spraying from a sheared cable in the side of the hole. In the glare, Milo saw how deep it went – right down into the bowels of the ship. And again he saw movement, tiny shapes far below.

'Did you see that?' he asked Lina. 'There's something down there.'

'I saw it,' Lina said. Then she raised her voice. 'Crater! I think you should get back here. We need light.'

'What about his power cells?' Milo asked.

'This is more important,' Lina told him. 'It's all too weird, we need to take a proper –'

The ship lurched suddenly beneath them, the floor tipping violently. Lina staggered and Milo reached for her, grabbing at her shirt. All around them he heard crates tottering and crashing.

The ship shook again and in the flash that followed Milo saw Lina falling. 'Milo!' she cried out, staggering back.

Milo tried to tighten his grip on her shirt, but the material tore and she tumbled into the ragged hole.

The ship righted itself, and the light faded. Lina was gone.

'Master Milo,' CR-8R said, coming up behind him. 'What happened? Where is Mistress Lina?'

'She fell!' Milo told him. 'Lina! Lina, can you hear me?'

CR-8R switched on his beams, flooding the hole with light. Milo heard a loud rustling sound, like the sound of hundreds of tiny feet scrabbling away on the deck below.

'Milo?' Lina's voice was distant and muffled, echoing up through the floor. 'Milo, where are you?'

'I'm right here,' he called back, peering down.

'I can't move,' Lina said. 'Milo, I'm stuck. And there's something down here. Something alive.'

'We have to get down there,' Milo told CR-8R. 'Can you float down and get her?'

'It would be a squeeze,' the droid said. 'And I won't leave you alone. Follow me, the steps are this way.'

'We're coming, Lina!' Milo called down. 'Just hold tight.'

'OK,' Lina said. 'But hurry.'

CR-8R kept his beams lit, leading Milo through the crates to the outer wall of the ship, which rose sheer and black ahead of them. In the wall was a dark opening and a winding staircase leading down.

CR-8R went ahead, but Milo found himself unable to move. He stood at the top of the steps with his heart pounding.

Memories flooded through him of a house they'd stayed in back on Tharl, an old wooden lodge his dad had borrowed between expeditions. Milo had loved everything about the place – except the basement. It had rickety, creaking steps, the lights never worked and it was filled with all kinds of critters and bugs, webs and dust. He used to stand at the top of the stairs and will himself to go down there – but he never could.

Well, he was older now, and braver. And besides, Lina was in trouble, and he wouldn't leave her. He swallowed his fear and started down.

CHAPTER 4

THE BASEMENT

Lina could feel something crawling up her leg. She tried to lie still, pressing her arms to her sides. Not that she could move very far anyway - she was wrapped in something smooth and sticky, the same substance CR-8R had found on the upper deck. The stuff was everywhere down here, great white webs threaded between the walls. One of them had broken her fall, but when she tried to clamber free she found herself stuck fast.

Sparks flared from the hole overhead and the thing on her leg froze, then began to move once more. It was joined by another, starting down at her foot and scuttling silently upwards. She craned her neck, feeling the sticky substance knotting in her hair.

She took a breath and tried to calm herself. If she stayed completely still, perhaps these creatures wouldn't hurt her. They had reached her stomach now, and she felt a cold, almost metallic touch on her skin as they scuttled across the exposed spot where her shirt had torn as she fell.

Then the flash came again, and Lina had to bite her tongue to stop herself from crying out. One of them hovered directly above her, a circular shape about the size of her hand. Eight legs jutted from it, gleaming silver. Black, segmented eyes reflected the sparks from above.

The creature was hanging by a fine thread, descending slowly but steadily towards her face. She saw tiny pincers snapping and heard the whir of microscopic gears.

Then the light was gone. Lina felt a wave of panic, knowing that any moment the spider would touch down, would brush her face with its thin little legs. She couldn't bear it.

She shook her head violently, trying to tug herself free. The other spiders were still climbing, tugging at her shirt as they scuttled closer, and still closer. She could feel more of them on her legs.

'Milo!' she cried out in terror. 'Where are you?'

Then suddenly the deck was flooded with light. CR-8R swept in, his beams on full power. Milo followed, his fists raised.

Lina heard a high-pitched squeal and saw the spider above her rising fast, legs writhing and tugging at the thread as it pulled itself back up. The silver skin on its back seemed to ripple and blister in the light, and she thought she saw a haze of smoke trailing from it. It vanished into the shadows, leaving a smell like scorched metal.

The other spiders had fled too, springing free and disappearing into fine cracks in the floor. Lina kicked and fought, managing to wrench one arm free.

CR-8R was using one of his lower appendages to slice through the webs strung across the deck, the sticky membranes clinging to him as he forced his way through. Milo followed, trying to steer clear of the hanging threads.

Then the droid was at Lina's side, and Milo was grabbing at her hand.

'Are you OK?' he asked.

'Just stuck,' Lina said. 'Did you see those spider-things? What were they?'

Milo shook his head. 'I've never seen anything like them,' he said. 'Can you get loose?'

Lina shook her head. 'It's really sticky.'

'Hold still, Mistress Lina' CR-8R said. 'I'm going to cut you down.'

Lina saw his appendage arm snaking up towards her, its cutting blade wreathed in sticky white web. She heard the snip of shears then she dropped suddenly, hitting the floor hard on her back.

'Oh, Mistress Lina, I'm so sorry!' CR-8R said. 'I really must be more careful.'

Lina tugged her other arm free and began to peel the webs from her clothes and hair. Her shirt and leggings glistened with gooey white threads and her hair was a tangled mess. She struggled to her feet, stamping and kicking.

CR-8R guided his glowlamps around the room, light piercing through the tangled forest of hazy cobwebs to the black walls behind. Milo let out a gasp. 'What happened here?'

The far side of the deck was a mass of pipes and machinery – Lina recognised cooling ducts and energy converters, and tall banks of power cells. But it all lay in twisted heaps, as though something had chewed the metal up and spat it out again. The cells were dead, their casings cracked and their steel innards strewn across the floor. And everything was covered in the same sticky white webbing.

'Well, I was right about there being a bug in the system,' Lina said. 'Lots of bugs, as it turns out. And they've been busy.'

'It's incredible,' Milo agreed. 'They feed on power and can chew through a plate-steel floor. It looked to me like they had metal skin.'

'Cyborgs?' CR-8R asked. 'But where can they have come from?'

Milo shrugged. 'A shipment?' he asked.

'We need to get to the bridge,' Lina said firmly. 'We can take a look at the Shade's records, figure out what she was carrying.'

'But keep your beams on this time, Crater,' Milo said. 'It looked to me like they're afraid of the light.'

'A fine plan,' CR-8R agreed. 'Provided my batteries hold out.'

'Well, what are we waiting for?' Lina asked. 'Let's move.'

They hurried back up the winding steps, CR-8R keeping his beams trained backwards so that Milo and Lina could stay in the light. As they climbed she could hear the spiders swarming back onto the darkened deck, reclaiming their territory.

They reached the top of the steps, weaving through the maze of crates. Many had been scattered when the gravity failed, and they had to clamber over a creaking, unsteady heap to reach the door.

'Look,' Milo said, pointing. Lying on its side at the top of the pile was a large container made of thick metal plates. It had been torn open, the steel twisted outwards as though something had forced its way free.

'Cylo,' Lina said, reading the word stencilled in heavy block letters on the side.

Then CR-8R's beams flashed one after another as he spun to face a heavy door set into the curved wall. He tapped in the code and the door slid open.

Lina ducked through, scanning the bridge. The only light came from outside the ship, the distant gleam of galactic centre like a pale river in the blackness. Below the viewscreen was a long control panel and four chairs. But the controls themselves were dead, and the room was silent.

She took a step forward, then froze. 'Hello?' she called out. 'Captain Mondatha, is that you?'

Sitting in the pilot's seat, her back turned to them, was a dark, robed figure.

CHAPTER 5

ON THE BRIDGE

'Hello?' Lina repeated.

The bounty hunter did not move, sitting upright in her chair, her hand on the controls.

Milo heard the door slide shut behind them. He followed Lina, stopping as he heard a crunch beneath his foot. He looked down. Something sticky and grey was oozing from under his shoe. He lifted it to see the flattened form of a spider, its metal body cracked to reveal gooey organic innards.

Another lay just ahead of it, flat on its back, eight legs in the air. He saw a third lying on the control panel.

Still the Captain did not move. Lina reached out, touching the Shade gently on the shoulder. She was stiff as a board, frozen in place. Lina gave a tug and the chair turned slowly.

The bounty hunter's head rocked back and Milo saw two red marks high on her neck, piercing the skin. The Shade clutched another of the spiders, crushed in her fist. But her eyes were

closed, her breathing shallow.

'She's unconscious,' Lina called. 'Those things must have attacked her.'

'And she must have fought back,' Milo said. 'Bad move.'

Lina pushed past the pilot's chair, tapping the console. Nothing happened. 'The navigation array's completely drained,' she said.

'Can you get it working?' Milo asked.

Lina shrugged. 'Everything seems to be intact, there's just no power. Crater, can you find out what those things were and what they might have done to the ship?'

The droid hovered towards the nearest energy socket, plugging himself in. 'I'll have to use my own power to access the data banks,' he said. 'Hopefully this won't take long.'

'Look for the most recent shipments,' Milo suggested.

'And the word Cylo,' Lina reminded him.

Milo perched in the co-pilot's chair. The air in the cockpit was cold and it tasted stale. The life-support systems must be failing like everything else. He wondered if they'd freeze before they ran out of air, or the other way around. No, he thought. Lina will figure out a way to fix it, like she always has before.

'I've found it,' CR-8R said. 'She picked up sixty crates, a week ago. She collected them from an Imperial research base, and the contact's name was Cylo.'

'So he's a person?' Milo asked.

'Or she,' Lina put in.

'A man, from what I can tell,' CR-8R said. 'The Shade did her research. Her notes say that Cylo is a research scientist working on ways to fuse the organic with the robotic to create new forms of life.'

'Sounds like our spiders,' Lina said.

'So they are cyborgs,' Milo said in amazement. 'Part robot, part animal.'

'And all dangerous,' Lina frowned. 'If one bite could take out the Shade, think what it could do to someone half her size.'

'She is still alive,' CR-8R said. 'That's positive.'

'But Lina, they never bit you,' Milo pointed out. 'Maybe they only attacked the Shade because she fought back.'

'Or maybe they're crazy little critters who love to suck human blood, when they're not crippling starships,' Lina said. 'We can't take any chances.

'Well, we know they hate the light,' Milo said. 'We can use that.'

'How?' Lina asked. 'All the lights are out.'

'No, they're not,' Milo reminded her. 'They were still working in the cell block.'

Lina frowned. 'You're right,' she said. 'And those holograms were still going too. Why haven't they run out of power? We saw the main power cells, they were chewed to bits. Everything on the ship ought to be dead.'

She scratched her forehead thoughtfully. Then Milo saw a light go on behind her eyes.

'Oh, this bounty hunter's smart,' she said with a grin. 'She's really smart. Think about it. On a regular freighter, the power cells are all stored in one place, right? The engine room. So if someone's attacking you, all they need to do is find that central source and knock it out, and you're dead in space.'

'I guess,' Milo agreed. He knew that the *Whisper Bird* had a single power grid controlling the whole ship. He had always assumed that was how all starships worked.

'But what if you split the power cells up into separate sources?' Lina asked. 'There'd be one for the bridge, that's obviously been knocked out, taking the navigation systems with it. There's another for the storage bay, and we saw how the spiders had dealt with that. But there must be another in the rear, powering the cell block. She must also have separated out the security system, which is why the holograms keep popping up. And there might even be another cell powering the hyperdrive.'

'So the ship could still fly?' Milo asked.

'I don't see why not,' Lina agreed. 'But there'd be no way to control it, we'd end up going in circles.' She screwed up her eyes, thinking hard. 'We'd need to get the navicomputer working. And for that we need another power source. There's only one we know of that's definitely still in operation.'

'Back at the cell block,' Milo put in.

'There was a box of tools back there,' Lina remembered. 'We uncouple the power cell, Crater carries it up here. We hook it up to the navigation array, and as long as we can keep the spiders out we'd probably have enough power to get back to Lothal.'

'Can you do that?' Milo asked excitedly. 'Unhook it, and rig it up?'

Lina's face fell. 'I honestly don't know,' she said. 'I've never tried to do anything like this before.'

'And I cannot promise my batteries will hold out,' CR-8R put in. 'I'm on backup power as it is.'

Lina frowned. She opened her mouth to speak, then she shut it again. 'There is another option,' she said at last. 'One other person around here who knows a thing or two about spaceship repair.

Everything there is to know, according to him.'

CR-8R shook his head. 'No,' he said flatly. 'Stel is a criminal. An outlaw. We don't even know what he's been locked up for.'

'But we can find out, can't we?' Lina pointed out. 'You could go back into the records and read his file.'

'Maybe all he's guilty of is stealing food for his family,' Milo suggested. 'Or punching a stormtrooper.'

'Or murder, or arson, or any number of horrendous crimes,' CR-8R shot back. 'He's not to be trusted.'

'So check the files and make sure,' Lina insisted. 'If you're going to have to power down soon anyway, we need to know who we can trust. We don't want to be out here alone.'

CR-8R sighed, hovering by the socket. Then he sighed again and plugged back in. 'Accessing confidential prisoner records,' he said. 'I'm afraid the files have become badly corrupted. Those spiders must have been chewing on the data cables.' His metal face darkened. 'Oh,' he said. 'Oh, dear me.'

He withdrew from the socket, frowning at the children. 'I'm afraid you're not going to like what I have to tell you,' he said.

'Just say it, Crater,' Lina snapped impatiently.

'One of those prisoners is just the man we're looking for,' CR-8R told them. 'He was imprisoned for hijacking an Imperial food transport and giving the proceeds to the poor. The other is... I can barely say it.'

'The butcher of Brentaal IV,' Milo said under his breath.

'Where did you hear that?' CR-8R asked.

'Stel told us,' Lina admitted. 'He said that was Davin's nickname. That's right, isn't it? Davin's the killer.'

'But that's just it,' CR-8R said. 'I don't know. One prisoner is a hero, the other a monster. But the files were so corrupted, I have no way of knowing which is which.'

Milo let out a short, startled laugh. 'Great,' he said.

Lina shook her head. 'But we do know,' she insisted. 'Stel told us about Davin. He gave Milo the food bar. He's been nothing but friendly since he came on board. Whereas Davin...'

'Looks like a total psycho,' Milo agreed.

'But how can we be sure?' CR-8R asked. 'What if this is all part of Stel's plan to make you trust him, to lull you into a false sense of security?'

Lina sighed. 'Why would he need our

trust?' she asked. 'He didn't know all this was going to happen. Look, I know we've made some poor choices recently. But I don't see how it could be any clearer. Either way, it's a risk I'm willing to take.'

She reached down to the Shade's belt, unclipping the bounty hunter's stun-stick. 'I'll take this just in case. Crater, where's that storage locker? We don't want her making trouble if she wakes up.'

'The locker is right outside that door,' CR-8R told her. 'But I don't think this...'

'We don't have a choice, Crater,' Lina insisted. 'Here, I'll take her feet, you get her arms. We'll lock her in, just like she did to us. Then we're going back to get Stel.'

They shoved the Shade inside the empty store cupboard and CR-8R used his welding attachment to melt the lock. Then they hurried back through the darkened cargo bay, the droid's fading beams lighting their way.

Lina could hear the rustle of the spiders all around them, could see their fleeting forms darting into the shadows. But she knew they wouldn't attack as long as she kept to the light.

The stun-stick in her hand lent her courage. Blue energy shimmered on the shaft, and she held it up in front of her, remembering her dad's stories about the brave Jedi and their lightsabers. This wasn't quite as impressive, but it was a start.

They passed the hole in the hangar floor, the spiders hurrying in and out on their own strange errands. The crates rose on either side and they picked up the pace, seeing the door at the far end standing open.

'Wait,' Milo said as they approached. 'Didn't we shut that?'

There was a crash from behind them

and Lina whipped round to see a stack of crates toppling to the floor. She heard a savage cry like an enraged animal. The crates rolled, spiders scattering frantically in all directions.

'Run!' she yelled, shoving Milo through the door. CR-8R followed, gliding as fast as he could down the steps and along the narrow corridor.

They could hear bellowing behind them, crashing and thumping and the thud of footsteps. Then they reached the door to the cell block, tumbling through it into the light.

CHAPTER 6

ON THE LOOSE

'What was that?' Milo asked breathlessly, screeching to a halt.

Lina slammed the panel and the door slid shut, sealing them in. 'I don't know,' she said. 'But it was big.'

'Mistress Lina...' CR-8R said.

Milo bent double, breathing hard. 'Could there be someone else on the ship?'

'Master Milo...' CR-8R tried.

Lina banged her fist on the solid steel door. 'Whatever it was, or whoever, they're not getting in here.'

'Hey, shut up and listen to your robot!' a voice snapped. 'He's trying to tell you something.'

They turned. Milo froze in horror. Lina gasped.

The gate to the far-end cell hung open, twisted almost off its hinges. The tin cup lay on the floor, crushed flat.

Stel leaned against the bars of his own cell, staring in amazement. 'I honestly didn't think he had the strength,' the young man told them. 'But he just kept pounding. Never said a word, just bang, bang, bang. I thought he was out of his mind, space crazy. Then I heard it snap.'

'This hinge,' CR-8R said, pointing. 'It was loose.'

'The stormtrooper,' Milo said, remembering. 'He threw him into the gate. That must have weakened it.'

Lina shivered, remembering the bellow they'd heard in the storage bay. Davin must have been so close, it was a miracle he hadn't caught them.

'I was going to ask him to free me too,'

Stel admitted. 'Then I saw the look in his eyes. There was nothing on that alien's mind but murder. That's when I knew where he was going.'

'Wh... where?' Milo asked.

'After you, of course,' Stel said.

'So why didn't he kill you?' Lina asked. 'He had the chance.'

Stel gave her a crooked smile. 'Maybe he likes me. Or maybe he just figured I wasn't going anywhere.'

'What do we do now?' Milo asked Lina. 'If we're trapped in here, what happens to your plan?'

'What plan?' Stel asked. 'You guys have a plan?'

Lina explained about the spiders, Stel's eyes lighting up as she told him about the separate power sources and her scheme to rig the cell-block battery to the navicomputer.

'Not a bad plan,' he said. 'She's a clever

one, that Shade, huh? Separate power cells, why didn't I ever think of –'

There was a thump behind them and Milo jumped. It came again, the heavy door into the cell block shuddering violently.

'He's come for us,' Lina said, trying to keep her voice steady. 'What do we do?' Dimly she thought she could hear shouting, as though the madman was calling out to them.

'I've got an idea,' Stel said. 'It's not as clever as yours, but...'

'Just tell us,' Lina pleaded, glancing back as the door rattled again.

'OK,' Stel said. 'You two kids get safe in the cells. The droid opens the door. Davin goes for you. I hide against the wall and hit him with that stunner. He goes down, we lock him up, everybody celebrates.'

Milo rolled his eyes. 'Why are we always the bait?' he groaned.

Stel laughed. 'If it makes you feel better, think of yourself as a distraction. You'll be safe in the cells. Me and the droid are the ones taking the risks.' He turned to Lina. 'What do you say, boss? Do I get the job?'

Lina gave him a thoughtful look. Then the thud came again and she nodded. 'Crater, let him out. It's the only way.'

CR-8R paused for a moment, unsure. Then he tapped in the code and the gate swung open.

Stel took a step into the hallway, a grin breaking across his face. 'You won't regret this,' he said. 'Now Lina, get in my cell. Milo, in yours. I'm not saying anything's going to go wrong, but if it does I'd feel safer if you weren't locked in together.'

Lina's heart hammered as the young convict swung both gates shut, sealing them in.

'And give me the stun-stick,' he said, reaching in to take it. He flicked the

switch, the rippling energy reflected in his green eyes. For a moment Lina thought she saw something else in there, something like hunger.

'OK, droid,' Stel said. 'You know what to do.'

CR-8R positioned himself by the door. 'Please be careful. We're all in a lot of danger if you miss your mark.'

'Don't sweat it, oilcan,' Stel grinned. 'I know what I'm doing. Besides, this guy's got no interest in droids. It's us he'll be after.'

He pressed himself against the wall, holding up one hand and counting down on his fingers.

Four, three... CR-8R reached for the panel. Stel raised the stun stick. Lina watched breathlessly.

Two, one... The door slid open. A huge figure loomed in the doorway, pausing for a moment before ducking inside. Davin towered over CR-8R, throwing the droid into shadow.

Then Lina noticed something that made her head spin. The big alien was smiling. He held his palms up as he stepped towards them, his eyes shining with what looked like relief.

'You're alive,' he said. 'I was –'

Stel leapt from hiding. There was a flash of blue light.

Davin fell like a tree, face first. His

forehead hit the deck with a crunch, right in front of Lina's cell.

Milo gripped the bars. 'Did you see his face?' he asked Lina. 'Something was wrong.'

'I know,' she called back. 'What was he trying to say?'

'He was probably trying to tell you how glad he was that you're OK,' Stel cut in. 'How thankful that I hadn't had the chance to hurt you. Yet.'

The young man spun on his heels, shoving the stun-stick at CR-8R. There was a spray of sparks and CR-8R reeled back. Electricity crackled as Stel thrust again, digging the stick furiously into the droid's side.

CR-8R shook, letting out a screech of impenetrable noise. His repulsors failed and he hit the floor, metal limbs jerking and twitching, appendages writhing like a nest of angry snakes.

Stel twirled the stun-stick around his hand like a baton. He drew back and dealt Davin a kick in the side, so hard that the Lasat's whole body shook. Then he turned to Milo and Lina.

'Surprise!' he said, and beamed at them.

Lina drew back, her hands clenched into fists. Stel's thin lips twitched excitedly and there was a wild gleam in his eyes.

'*You're* the butcher of Brentaal IV,' Milo

said. 'It was you all along.'

'That's what they called me,' Stel admitted. 'The things I did, sometimes I can't even believe it was me. But that was a long time ago. I'm better now. Sort of.'

'So why did you lie to us?' Lina asked. 'Why did you say it was Davin?' She gestured to the snoring body face-down at her feet.

'Because I wanted you to like me and hate him,' Stel said. 'I like to be liked. Doesn't everyone?'

He placed one foot on Davin's back. The alien grunted but did not wake. 'He came here for you, of course,' Stel said, taking a step up and balancing on Davin's motionless form. 'He was sent to get you out. But he couldn't say so in front of me. He was smart, you see. He never trusted me for a moment.'

'How do you know what he was up to?' Milo asked. 'How do you know he came to rescue us?'

Stel snorted. 'Have you really not figured it out?' he spat. 'I was on the run for years, that part was true. Those senators put a price on my head so big, I knew it was only a matter of time before someone caught up with me. But then the Republic was gone. And when the stormtroopers came knocking, they weren't there to arrest me.'

'You're working for the Empire,' Lina gasped. 'But you're a killer.'

'Exactly,' Stel laughed. 'I was just the kind of person they were after. Someone who could do the things even their troopers couldn't. And the first mission they gave me was him.'

He bounced on his heels, grinning cruelly. 'I tracked him to Lothal, then I called in the stormtroopers and they snatched him up,' he said. 'But when I heard the orders had been changed, that he wasn't going to face trial in Capital City but would be shipped to Noctu by some bounty hunter... I knew something was up. I told them to lock me up right along with him.'

'How would that help?' Lina asked. 'Why didn't you just order the Shade to bring him back?'

'Because I have no doubt that when we get to Noctu, he'll have a ship waiting,' Stel grinned. 'So I don't just get him, I get everyone he's working with. It's a brilliant plan, if I do say so myself. And it would've worked perfectly if it wasn't for those cursed spiders.'

There was a groan of gears and Lina looked to see CR-8R picking himself up, tipping as his repulsors faltered then kicked back in. 'Are either of you hurt?' he asked.

'You've only been out for a few moments,' Lina said. 'Just long enough for us to find out this one's working for the Empire. Davin's the real rebel.'

CR-8R hung his head. 'I did try to warn you,' he said. 'I assume he's expecting Davin to lead him to his people. Which means there'll be an Imperial transport waiting for us when we reach the asteroid mines.'

Stel clapped appreciatively. 'Bolt-bucket here's not as dumb as he looks,' he said. 'I honestly had no idea who any of you were when I came on board. All I knew was that there were two kids and a droid, and that I wasn't to let any of them escape. They didn't say anything about bringing you in alive, though.'

'You lay one hand on them,' CR-8R said, 'and I'll –'

'You'll what, chrometop?' Stel cut him off. Then he sighed. 'I need the girl to help me fix the navicomputer. And I need the boy to keep her in line. So don't get your circuits in a bunch. For now, you're all safe.'

He looked down. 'There is one thing you can do for me, though,' he said. 'Get this lump of meat back where he belongs.'

'I refuse to take orders from the likes of you,' CR-8R said firmly, crossing his arms.

'Fine.' Stel marched to Milo's cell. 'Come here, kid. This won't hurt. Much.' He thrust the stun-stick through the bars.

'Very well!' CR-8R protested. 'I'll do as you ask.' He took hold of Davin's ankles and dragged him towards the nearest cell.

'Right inside,' Stel ordered. 'I know he's heavy, but look at those arms. Load-lifter, right? Now get back here, and make sure you lock it.'

CR-8R did as he was told, tapping in the code. Stel pushed past him, grabbing the gate and giving it a good shake.

'Seems secure,' he said. 'I guess he could try and smash his way out again, but not before we get where we're going. Now, if you'd also be so kind as to unlock the

girl's cell.'

CR-8R hesitated but Stel shook the stun-stick at him. Lina stepped cautiously into the corridor, taking CR-8R's arm.

'Your plan was good,' Stel told her. 'I've decided to stick to it, with a few modifications. But I'll need you up on the bridge, I'm guessing another pair of hands will come in useful.'

'I'll never help you,' Lina spat.

Stel shrugged. 'Fine,' he said. 'The Empire will retrace our course and find us eventually. I'm sure I'll be able to find a fun way to pass the time until they do.' And he fingered the switch on the stun-stick, the blue light flickering off and on.

Lina stared at him. She knew this was all her fault. If she hadn't been so sure he was trustworthy none of it would've happened. All she could do now was play for time, and hope Davin's people were heavily armed.

'So how do we find the power cell?' she asked.

'We don't need it,' Stel told her. 'We've got a portable power source right here.' And he jerked a thumb at CR-8R.

'I'm afraid that won't work,' the droid told him. 'I'm running on emergency power already.'

'Then I'll drain what's left and figure it out from there,' Stel snapped. 'I don't have time to go tearing up the floor searching for the source when all I need is enough juice to run the navicomputer. Once we're on our way you can shut down.'

'And what about me?' Milo piped up.

'You stay here,' the young man told him. 'And remember, I have your sister.' He smiled, clicking his heels. 'Right, let's move. The girl first, then the droid, then me.'

'We'll be back,' Lina promised Milo as she stepped out into the corridor. 'Just sit tight.'

'Be careful,' Milo called out. 'Don't do anything risky, OK?'

Lina forced a smile. 'Who, me?'

Then she was gone.

CHAPTER 7

SPIDERS

'Wake up!' Milo shouted, rattling the bars as hard as he could. 'Please, wake up!'

Davin lay on the floor of the far-end cell, arms splayed at his sides. He twitched, grunted and reached up to scratch his nose. Then he settled back and began to snore, his great bulk rising and falling.

Milo sank against the bars, letting out a cry of frustration. Too much time had passed since Stel had marched Lina and CR-8R back to the bridge. His sister could take care of herself, he knew that. But he also knew that Stel was not to be trifled with; he'd seen the mad gleam in the young man's eyes.

The door leading out of the cell block stood open, the corridor beyond still in darkness. A moment ago Milo had thought he saw movement out there, low to the ground. And if he held his breath and listened hard, he could hear the scuttling of tiny feet.

The spiders had been drawn by the power source in the cell block. But as long as the ceiling light was working there was no way for them to enter.

A thought started to form in his mind. But before he could latch onto it he heard a groan. Davin was trying to lift himself up.

'Yes!' Milo cried out. 'That's right, Davin. You can do it.'

The Lasat shook his vast dome of a head, reaching up with one fist to lever himself off the floor. 'I'm up,' he moaned.

'Leave me alone, mother. I won't be late.'

Then he rolled over and sat up, blinking. His head lolled, eyes straining to focus. They fixed on the boy, and Milo saw a gleam of realisation beneath his huge protruding forehead.

'What happened?' Davin asked, his voice slurred and booming. 'What's going on?'

'Stel took my sister,' Milo explained. 'He's the villain, not you.'

'So you worked it out,' the alien said, grasping the bars to pull himself up.

'Sorry,' Milo said. 'He seemed... nicer.'

'Teach you not to go on looks,' Davin grunted, rubbing his head. 'He hit me with that stunner. Again.'

Milo nodded. 'He said you wanted to hurt us,' he said. 'So we let him knock you out. Then he told us the truth.'

'Imperial,' Davin said. 'I could smell it on him. That's why I couldn't say why I came here. Truth is, the Bridgers sent me.'

'I hoped they had,' Milo said warmly. 'But listen, we're in a bad spot. Stel's found a way to get the ship running again. When we reach Noctu, the Empire will be waiting.' And he told him everything that had happened, from the spiders to Stel's betrayal.

'Then there's no time to waste,' Davin said when Milo had finished. Davin gave the bars of his cell a powerful shake, the steel groaning beneath his fists. But the gate did not budge.

Davin snarled. 'The last one had a weak hinge. This one's solid as rock. If only I had a stormtrooper to throw at it.'

'I have an idea,' Milo admitted. 'I haven't completely thought it through, but I think it'll work. Can you reach that?'

He gestured to the flattened tin cup,

discarded in the hallway between the cells. Davin got down on his knees, straining between the bars. The muscles in his arm stood out like twisted vines. He grabbed once, twice, then took hold and pulled the battered cup towards him.

'OK,' he said, climbing to his feet. 'I've got it. Now what?'

'You see that panel by the door?' Milo asked. 'The Shade told us it was a light switch. I need you to turn it off.'

'Why?' Davin grimaced. 'Then we'll be sat in the dark.'

'The only way to get out of these cells is to power down the locks,' Milo explained. 'And there's only one way I can see to make that happen.'

He glanced back towards the open doorway. Tiny shapes writhed and scuttled in the darkness beyond.

Davin's mouth dropped. 'You're not serious,' he said. 'I've heard some crazy ideas, but letting in a load of cyborg spiders... I won't do it.'

'I'm sure they won't bite unless we provoke them,' Milo insisted. 'We just need to stand perfectly still and let them do their work.'

But Davin shook his head. 'You don't know that,' he said. 'And I can't stand spiders. They give me the shivers, ever since I was a kid.'

Milo couldn't help smiling. 'You're scared,' he said in amazement. 'I guess everyone's frightened of something, but I thought you...'

'Thought I what?' Davin demanded. 'I may look tough. OK, I am tough. But that don't mean I want creepy crawlies running all over me.'

'Well this is the only plan we've got,' Milo said. 'If it works we could get up to the bridge before Stel can get the hyperdrive working. But if you're too much of a coward...'

Davin growled, deep in his throat. Then he spat on the floor. 'All right,' he said. 'But if one of those things sinks its fangs into me, it'll be your fault.'

He leaned out as far as he could, clutching the cup. Milo held his breath as Davin tested his aim. Then the alien threw the cup as hard as he could. There was a crash and the lights went out.

'Nice shot!' Milo called out.

Davin snorted. 'Thanks,' he said. 'Now what?'

'Now we stay very still,' Milo told him. 'And listen.'

At first he could hear only one set of tiny feet, barely audible as the first spider scuttled tentatively into the cell block. Then he heard another one following, and another. The tapping turned to a rattling rush as the tiny creatures swarmed across the metal deck plates.

'I really don't like this,' Davin whispered in the darkness.

'Just stay still,' Milo said. 'I swear, they won't hurt you.' He bit his lip, hoping he was right.

Then Davin let out a moan of discomfort. 'I can feel them on me,' he muttered fearfully. 'On my legs. They're climbing up.'

'Just breathe,' Milo told him. 'Try to think about something else.'

The Lasat snorted. 'I'll think about how I'm never doing another favour for those Bridgers,' he said.

Now Milo could feel them too, like tiny fingers grasping at his trousers. It almost tickled, but he didn't feel like laughing. He stood as still as he could, feeling them reach his shirt, thankful that he'd remembered to tuck it in. They won't hurt you, he repeated to himself.

They're just friendly little creatures, they won't hurt you...

Then one of them brushed against his neck and he had to fight to keep from crying out. His hands were shaking and he balled his fists, slipping them into his pockets.

Suddenly a voice cut the silence and the room rippled with pale-blue light. 'Stop, prisoner!' the Shade's hologram demanded. 'Any attempt to escape will be met with retaliatory force!'

It stood in the centre of the hallway, one hand raised. 'Return to your cells!' it shouted. 'Return immediately!'

In the shimmering light Milo could see Davin in the far cell, a huge, motionless shadow. The light shifted, and for one wild moment Milo thought the alien had put on some kind of metal suit. Then he realised – he was covered from head to toe in spiders. They

swarmed all over him in rippling
silver waves.

'Wow, they really seem to like you,'
Milo called out. There were three
spiders on his own shirt, one in his hair
and a couple more on his legs, but for
the most part they seemed to be leaving
him alone.

'Great,' Davin's strangled voice

emerged from the gleaming mass. 'How do I get them to stop?'

'Be quiet!' the hologram barked. 'Everyone, silence!'

'It's weird,' Milo agreed. 'Why would they go for you like this?'

'I should have said before,' Davin said sheepishly. 'I took a laser blast in the chest, years back. The medibots fitted me with a metal lung. Must have its own power source.'

Suddenly there came a rising hum from the far end of the cell, like a motor charging. Peering sideways, Milo could see the spiders swarming around one particular panel on the floor, clambering over one another in their eagerness to reach it. They began to dig into the deck, using their sharp pincers to tear at the metal.

The spider in his hair scuttled free and dropped to the floor. He could feel the others doing the same, hurrying towards the source of the sound.

'They've found the power cell,' he whispered. 'Shouldn't be too long now. I hope.'

'You'd better be right,' Davin muttered, his voice muffled. 'Because I think they... oh no, this one's trying to get in my mouth.' He spat, and Milo heard something hit the floor.

'Be careful,' he warned. 'Don't spook them.'

The spiders had chewed a hole in the floor of the cell block. They swarmed into it, the hum of electricity rising and falling as they began to drain the power.

'You don't...' Davin said, following Milo's gaze. 'You don't think they'll try and do that to me, do you?'

Milo didn't know what to say. The spiders wanted energy, they didn't care where it came from. If they figured out there was a source inside Davin, they'd do whatever they could to get at it.

'I don't –' he started. But before he could finish, the lights in the ceiling flickered on, pulsed for a moment, then died once again. With a click, the cell gate swung open.

'Stop!' the hologram barked as Milo stepped out cautiously, crossing the hallway. 'Get back! Stay where you are! Move along!'

Milo crossed to the other cell, peering up at the gleaming silver shape looming over him. He reached up carefully, taking one of the spiders between his fingers as carefully as he could. He could see its little legs waving madly, pincers snapping. He dropped it and the spider scampered away towards the power source.

Milo reached for another spider, and another. Soon Davin's head was uncovered, his wide eyes staring at Milo as the boy picked the spiders off one by one. Soon Davin was able to join in, plucking the spiders carefully from his skin and clothes.

He looked down at Milo and smiled ruefully. 'It was a good plan,' he said. 'You're a clever kid.'

'And you're very brave,' Milo replied, then he blushed. 'Sorry, that's just what my mum always used to say to me.'

But the alien was grinning. 'Mine too,' he said. 'Come on, let's get out of here.'

Milo walked on his tiptoes, placing his feet carefully. The spiders were still swarming through the doorway, streaming along the hall towards the hole at the far end. He clung to the door frame, swinging himself out. Then Davin followed, taking huge strides.

They crept along the corridor towards the steps. There was a sudden clang and

Davin muttered an apology. He reached down.

'Hey look, a hydrospanner,' he said. 'Could be useful.'

'You can do ship repairs?' Milo asked.

'No,' Davin admitted. 'But they're great for hitting people over the head with.'

Milo grinned. They'd get up to the bridge, find Lina and stop Stel before it was too late.

Then he felt the floor beneath his

feet begin to vibrate. The ship creaked around them. He clutched onto Davin's arm, struggling to keep his balance as he felt his stomach roll over.

They had jumped to lightspeed.

CHAPTER 8

A TRAP

Stel grinned at Lina as the ship rocketed into hyperspace. 'You see?' the young convict said, angling the pilot's chair towards her. 'I told you we'd have enough juice. Thanks to that droid of yours.'

CR-8R had propped himself against the console behind them, half sitting, half lying with a thick cable running from the side of his neck into the navicomputer. He could no longer keep himself upright after the power had been drained from his repulsors.

Lina knelt at the droid's side. 'How are you feeling, Crater?' she asked.

CR-8R stirred, raising his head slowly. There was no light in his golden eyes. 'SSSSSSSllllllllleeeeeeeee ppppppppppyyyyyyyyy,' he managed in a deep, slurred rumble. Then he slumped back down.

Lina wondered if droids ever dreamed, sparks of stray computer code sending messages through their cybernetic consciousness. If so, CR-8R had never mentioned it.

She let go of the droid's limp hand, frowning up at Stel. 'If he's got any permanent damage, I'll –'

'You'll what?' Stel snapped. 'I did what I had to do, didn't I? Besides, it's only a droid. Stop trying to make me feel guilty.'

He put his feet up on the control panel, rocking back in his chair and watching the spiralling tunnel of light wrap around the *Moveable Feast* as they plunged through hyperspace.

Lina got to her feet, glancing back towards the door that led to the storage bay. It was sealed tight to keep the spiders out, but Stel had made CR-8R tell them the code so Lina knew she could get out if she needed to. But what would be the point? Milo was safer where he was, and Stel would catch her if she tried to run.

She returned to the co-pilot's chair, tripping over CR-8R's outstretched leg. Her elbow slammed into the starboard control panel and Lina took a sharp breath as lights rippled across it: a row of coloured touchpads and a tiny independent viewscreen.

Stel craned his neck and Lina leaned over hurriedly, covering the panel with her arm.

'What are you doing back there?' her captor sneered.

'Nothing,' Lina said breezily. 'I tripped.' She gave her elbow a rub, and winced for good measure.

Stel shook his head. 'Try to be more careful.'

Lina slipped out of her jacket, tossing it casually over the lighted panel. Then she sank into the seat next to Stel, trying to keep the grin off her face. Somehow, the *Moveable Feast*'s weapons systems were still operational. And even better, Stel had no idea.

It made sense, she supposed – the exterior cannons would be on the same power grid as the security holograms. Their source must be so well hidden that even the spiders hadn't stumbled across it. She wasn't sure what she'd do with this knowledge, but she was determined to turn it to their advantage.

'So what are the Empire after you kids for, anyway?' Stel asked, yawning deeply.

Lina drew her knees up to her chin. 'They took our parents,' she said. 'We've been trying to get them back.'

'That's not really a reason,' he said, fingering the handle of the stun-stick clipped to his waist. 'I figure it has something to do with the droid. But hey, it's none of my business. All I need to do is hand you all over and pick up my next assignment.'

Lina scanned his pale face. 'You really enjoy this, don't you?'

Stel opened one eye and smiled. 'I really do,' he said. 'I used to hate the old Republic. All those stuffy, know-it-all senators and pompous Jedi, going around thinking they were better than everyone else. It's not like that with the Empire.'

'Of course it is,' Lina snarled. 'The Empire think they have the right to tell us all what to do and what to think, to lock us up, to steal people away...'

'Well, maybe they're right,' Stel said. 'Did you think about that? Maybe they do know what's best. They're bringing order, justice and peace.'

'You don't believe in all that,' Lina said. 'You just go along with it because they give you an excuse to push people around, and worse.'

Stel shrugged. 'Maybe so,' he said. 'It's good, though. Feeling like you're part of something. Now, if I get the urge to do something bad, I know the Empire will forgive me. They might even pay me for it.'

Lina shuddered, turning her face away. She wondered how many monsters like Stel were free to roam the galaxy now that the Empire were in charge. And how many good people like her parents were locked away, helpless.

A light on the main panel began to

flash and Lina heard the hum of the hyperdrive changing pitch.

'We're coming up on Noctu,' Stel said. 'Get ready, now.'

The vortex dissipated as they dropped out of lightspeed. Long shadows filled the bridge.

Lina could see Noctu's star up ahead, a distant disc no bigger than her fingernail. The planet off the starboard side offered a little more light, gleaming a pale, watery blue.

And between the ship and the planet, Lina could see the bustling hive of the Noctu mines. They called it an asteroid field but it was really a planetary ring, a disc of ice and boulders circling the massive gas giant. Some of the particles were smaller than snowflakes while others were ship-sized, spinning in endless orbit. Around the largest of these she saw transports buzzing like insects,

carrying men and machinery.

'Did you know all this used to be a moon?' Stel asked. 'It's true. Stel knows things. Centuries ago this was Noctu's biggest and richest moon, crammed to the core with minerals, gems, spice, you name it. But they dug too deep, those old ones. And one day, boom! The whole moon exploded. This ring is all that's left.'

'Didn't stop them mining though, did

it?' Lina pointed out.

Stel shook his head. 'The Republic closed the place down, too dangerous,' he said. 'But the Empire opened it up again. Now they use convict labour, just like on Kessel. They say fifty men die every week working out here. I almost feel bad for old Davin.'

Lina glared. 'I hate the Empire,' she said. 'And I hate you.'

Stel grinned. 'I know you do, sweetheart.'

An alarm sounded and Stel sat upright. 'Here we go,' he said. 'Let's hope the droid's got enough power left to run the comlink.'

'*Moveable Feast*,' a voice came rattling through the speakers. 'This is the commercial freighter *Sunburst*. Do you copy?'

Stel put one hand on the comlink, drawing the stun-stick from his belt.

'Answer them,' he said softly. 'And don't do anything stupid.'

Lina could see the freighter approaching, silhouetted against the distant sun. It was a battered old G9 Rigger, with a square central frame and two rusty wings at right angles. Lina scanned the horizon for the Imperial craft she knew was out there, but could see nothing.

She pushed the transmission button. '*Sunburst*, this is *Moveable Feast*,' she said. 'We copy loud and clear.'

'What's your status, *Feast*?' the voice replied. 'Who am I speaking to?'

Lina looked at Stel, who nodded slowly. 'This is Lina Graf,' she said, her hand trembling on the com panel.

There was a sigh of relief. 'Lina,' the voice said. 'This is Mira Bridger. Are you and Milo safe? Is Davin with you?'

Lina bit her lip. 'He's busy,' she said.

'He went to... get something.'

Stel grabbed her arm, warning her with his eyes.

'What do you mean?' Mira's voice came back. 'Went where? Lina, is everything OK?'

'Everything's fine,' Lina said through gritted teeth as Stel's fingers dug into her elbow. Her heart was racing and her vision was blurred, tears welling in her eyes.

Then for the briefest moment she saw it, a faint shadow passing across the planet's face and turning towards them. A boxy body and curved wings. The Imperial troop ship.

'Get out of here!' she shouted before she could stop herself. 'Mira, run, it's a trap!'

Stel roared, lashing out with the stun-stick. Lina threw herself sideways out of the chair, hitting the floor hard.

She heard him swing the stick, heard it strike the chair as she clambered away, dragging herself towards the door.

Stel jumped to his feet, coming for her. Lina rolled onto her back, pulling herself up into a sitting position. She knew that if she tried to stand he'd lash out, and this time he wouldn't miss.

The young man paused, running a hand through his flame-red hair. One hand flicked the switch on the stun-stick restlessly. Behind him Lina could see the *Sunburst* banking rapidly, running lights gleaming as it turned. The Imperial ship was closing in. As Lina watched it began to fire, laser blasts rippling across the rear of the freighter.

Then to her right, inside the cockpit, she saw movement. Lina blinked twice, to show she understood.

Stel took another step, looming over her. 'You can run, but it won't make any

difference,' he said. 'My Imperial friends
will blow that pitiful rebel craft out of
the sky.'

'You're wrong,' Lina said, craning her
neck. 'They're already firing back. Oh,
great shot!'

Stel shook his head, standing firm.
'Nice try,' he said. 'But I don't distract
easily. What were you going to do, grab
my ankle, try to pull me down? You really
are a child.'

'You're clever,' Lina told him. 'That's exactly what was supposed to happen. Only I wasn't the one doing the grabbing.'

Stel's eyes widened as CR-8R took hold of his leg, giving a hard tug. The convict let out a cry as he lost his balance. Lina jumped to her feet, giving him a shove. Stel flew back, landing hard in the pilot's chair. CR-8R slumped back, his last energy reserves drained.

Lina sprinted for the door, tapping in the code. She could hear Stel getting to his feet behind her, heard him lunge towards her as she flung herself through.

She hit something huge and soft, and staggered back.

'Hello Lina,' Davin said with a grin. Then he reached out and grabbed Stel by the neck, lifting him off his feet.

CHAPTER 9

ONE GOOD SHOT

Stel kicked wildly as he was hauled off the floor, his face reddening as Davin's hand tightened around his throat. The Lasat snarled, his scarred face grimacing in the light from the open doorway. Stel gasped for air, his eyes bulging.

Milo grabbed Davin's free hand. 'Don't,' he said. 'Please. Let him live.'

Davin looked at Milo and his face softened.

Summoning his strength, Stel swung the stun-stick towards Davin's face. The alien let go in surprise. Stel dropped, landing smartly on both feet.

Davin pulled the hydrospanner from his pocket, blocking Stel's next thrust. Bolts of wild energy were flung from the shaft of the stun-stick, casting both their faces in stark blue light.

'Are you OK?' Milo asked his sister.

Lina nodded. 'I see you've been making friends.'

They jerked back as Stel lunged again with the stun-stick, at the same time

kicking hard at Davin's ankle. The alien staggered, wincing. Stel thrust forward and Davin countered, but he was driven back into the shadows of the storage bay. He slammed into a stack of crates which toppled noisily all around him.

Milo and Lina watched breathlessly as Stel charged through the rain of crates, elbowing them aside. Stel swung his stun-stick and Davin blocked with his spanner. Stel was smaller and not as powerful, but his lightning thrusts kept catching the large alien off guard.

Davin grunted as he countered another blow, the stun-stick hammering down, knocking the hydrospanner from his hand. Davin looked down in surprise, then Stel lashed out again. Davin swung around to block with his fist, realising too late what that meant.

'Oh, not again,' he cried as the gleaming tip of the stun-stick slammed into his hand.

The stun-stick flew from Stel's grasp, skittering across the floor of the hangar. Davin toppled back into the wall of crates. Then he slumped to the floor, a look of annoyance on his face.

Milo threw himself down on the deck, grabbing for the stun-stick. Stel was right on top of him, and Milo felt a foot on his back as he grasped the handle. The breath was forced from his body.

'Get away from him!' Lina cried, shoving at Stel. The convict staggered back and Milo leapt up, brandishing the stun-stick.

Stel retreated, holding up his hands. 'Think about what you're doing, kid,' he said. 'You don't want to be hasty.'

Milo lashed out, trails of blue energy flashing in the darkness. 'Get back,' he cried.

Stel retreated into the maze of crates, his eyes fixed on the boy. 'Just put that down and we can talk,' he said. 'I don't want to hurt you, or your sister.'

'Don't listen to him, Milo,' Lina said, close at his shoulder. 'Everything he says is a lie.'

Milo stepped over Davin's slumped form, keeping the stun-stick raised. 'You're a traitor,' he told Stel. 'And a murderer. Why should we believe anything you say?'

'I gave you a food bar!' the young man whimpered pitifully. 'I'm not all bad! Am I?'

Milo barked a laugh. 'What do you want, a medal?'

They could hear the rustling all around them, the tapping of tiny feet as the spiders closed in. From the corner of his eye Milo saw their tiny shapes swarming over the toppled crates.

Stel backed around a corner, his pitiful stare turning to a snarl of fury. 'You'll pay for this,' he said. 'Little brats, you'll both pay. The Empire is greater than you, greater than me, greater than everything. They'll rule this galaxy for a thousand years.'

'You're wrong,' Milo said, lashing out. 'They'll fall, and so will you.'

Stel stumbled backwards. The spiders had been hard at work – the hole in the deck was twice the size it had been, a great ragged gulf opening onto darkness.

The convict cried out as he fell, clutching vainly at the edges of the hole. Then he was gone, sparks flying as he vanished from sight.

Lina hurried up behind Milo, watching as the spiders swarmed into the breach. There was a distant shriek, then silence.

'They're just protecting their nest,' Milo said. 'Once he stops kicking they'll leave him alone.'

They made for the cockpit, using the stun-stick to light their way. Milo almost tripped over Davin's body, kneeling at his side. 'We can't leave him for the spiders,' he said. 'Not after he came all this way to help us. Get his ankles, I'll take this end.'

They dragged Davin towards the cockpit door, pulling and pushing. They'd just managed to drag him inside when there was a deafening boom and the *Moveable Feast* juddered forcefully.

Lina's face dropped. 'I almost forgot,' she said. 'Milo, the Bridgers are here. The Empire have them pinned down. But I think I know how we can help.'

In the distance they could see the pale blue planet and the ring of asteroids surrounding it. The battered freighter was a lot nearer, spewing steam as it limped away from them.

The Imperial ship swung into view overhead, weapons firing as it closed in. It was in much better shape, firing another volley as it pursued the freighter, gaining fast.

Lina slipped into the co-pilot's seat, activating the weapons panel. Lights flickered across the display and Milo heard gears grinding somewhere above them.

Then he spotted CR-8R, slumped lifeless on the floor. 'Oh no, what happened?' he cried out, kneeling at the droid's side.

'He'll be OK once we get to a power socket,' Lina said, staring down at the panel in front of her, her eyes wide with worry. 'Right now I really need to figure out how all this works.'

Milo came up behind her, watching closely. Lina spread out her palms on either side of the panel, sliding them back and forth. A circle in the centre of the viewscreen marked the firing window, and Lina struggled to line it up with the enemy craft.

'One good shot,' she muttered to herself. 'Just one, to disable their weapons.'

'Have you done this before?' Milo asked.

Lina shook her head. 'But I watched Dad that time, remember? When those pirates came after us on Chankin.'

'That was years ago!' Milo countered. 'And the systems on the *Bird* might be totally different. If you hit the wrong ship, we really are done for.'

Lina shifted her hands, trying to lock the target circle onto the Imperial craft's rear engines. Milo held his breath, his knuckles white on the back of her chair. The target drifted, centred for a moment then drifted again. Lina cursed, gritting her teeth.

The freighter began to turn and Milo saw a flash of light as the port-side engine shorted out, spraying hot metal out into space. The Imperial craft fired again, shots glancing across the freighter's bow.

Then Lina let out a yell as the target locked on, the circle flashing red. She slammed her fist down on the panel and Milo felt the *Moveable Feast* shake around them. Laser bolts flashed overhead, gleaming white. He grabbed Lina's hand.

Both bolts struck the Imperial craft dead centre, flames rippling outward. The starboard engine erupted, taking the main gun port with it. The ship began to roll, spitting fire as it tumbled away from the fleeing freighter.

Lina leapt to her feet, grabbing Milo

as hard as she could. Over her shoulder
he could see the Imperial craft, thrusters
firing as she struggled to right herself.

Then in the light of the far-off sun he
saw the old freighter turning, leaving a
trail of sparkling dust as it limped back
towards them. He breathed a deep sigh

of relief and let himself be hugged.

CHAPTER 10

TRANSMISSION

Mira Bridger knelt beside Davin, shining a small torch into one eye, then the other. 'Twice would be unfortunate,' she said. 'But getting yourself knocked out three times? That's just careless.'

The Lasat grunted irritably, swaying in his seat and struggling to focus.

'He saved our lives, though,' Milo said, putting a hand on Davin's arm. 'So hopefully it was worth it.'

'That it was,' Ephraim Bridger said, crossing the low cargo bay of the *Sunburst*. He smiled down at the children, his eyes twinkling. 'Now let's

get out of here before he has to do
it again.'

As the cockpit door slid open Lina
looked up. Past Ephraim's retreating
back she could see the *Moveable Feast*
still adrift in space, a lifeless grey hulk
receding as they powered away. The
wounded Imperial transport had drawn
closer and was attempting to lock onto
the Shade's ship.

Lina slapped her head. 'We totally
forgot,' she said. 'Captain Mondatha.
She's still stuck in that store cupboard!'

'Let her rot there,' Davin snarled.

'I'm sure the stormtroopers will let
her out,' Mira said. 'Though I don't know
how this Captain Korda will react when
he finds out you two got away. And his
precious Crater, too.'

The droid lay against the wall,
plugged into the nearest power socket.
He was still groggy, but Lina could see

light slowly seeping back into his golden eyes.

'Who do you think's going to be in the most trouble,' Milo grinned. 'Stel, or the Shade?'

'They'll all be in trouble if those spiders jump ship,' Lina laughed. 'Honestly, they were the worst.'

'They weren't so bad,' Milo said. 'They were just doing what spiders do. Finding food and a warm place to nest.'

Davin shuddered. 'If I never see one of those critters again in my life, it'll be too soon,' he said, reaching up to scratch his enormous bald head. 'Honestly, when they were all over me I thought that was it. I thought I'd never – aagh!'

He let out a scream, jumping up on his chair with panic on his face. From his shirt pocket protruded a pair of shiny silver legs.

The alien reached out, clearly

intending to punch himself in the chest. But before he could make a move the spider had sprung free and was scampering down his leg.

'Get it!' Milo shouted, moving to cut the creature off.

Lina leapt for it, stamping with both feet. The spider wove between them, fleeing desperately.

'Don't let it get away,' Mira called out.

'Watch it, there it goes!'

The spider doubled back, legs skittering. A panel in the wall had been removed for repairs, exposing the ship's innards. If the spider made it that far, Lina knew they'd never be able to catch it without taking the *Sunburst* to pieces.

Milo threw himself down but the creature scuttled free of his grasping hands. Lina watched in horror as it closed the distance to the loose panel, preparing to spring.

Then a dark shape bounded out of nowhere, leaping on the spider and snatching it up with long-clawed hands. Morq stuffed the spider ravenously into his beak and swallowed. Lina saw a pair of silver legs jutting from the Kowakian monkey-lizard's mouth, then it was gone.

'Morq!' Milo cried out joyfully, opening his arms wide. The little monkey-lizard sprang into them,

nuzzling his beak against the boy's neck. 'Why didn't you tell me he was on board?' Milo asked Mira.

'We didn't know,' Mira admitted. 'He must have stowed away. Crafty little critter.'

Milo clutched Morq to him, and Lina couldn't remember the last time she'd seen her brother so happy. Perhaps their luck was starting to change.

She looked up at Mira, who was watching the boy with kind eyes.

'Thanks for coming to get us,' Lina said. 'I mean, I know you came for Crater too, and what's in his head. But you saved our lives. We'll never be able to repay you.'

Mira shook her head. 'You'll never have to,' she said. 'And we didn't come for Crater. Or at least we did, because we like him. But we like you, too. Us rebels have to stick together, right?'

'Right,' Lina said.

'Now you should both sit down, because I have something to tell you,' Mira went on. Milo did as she asked. Morq perched on his shoulder, chattering to himself.

'We're on our way back to Lothal,' Mira told them. 'Just before we left, we received a transmission from a friend of ours with connections inside the Empire. He thinks he may know where they're keeping your parents.'

Lina took Milo's hand. She opened her mouth but nothing came. Could it be true?

She looked up at Mira, who smiled and nodded slowly. 'I believe this is a good lead,' she said. 'You should believe it too.'

There was a shout from the cockpit. 'Buckle up back there,' Ephraim called out. 'I'm about to make the jump to lightspeed.'

Lina's hands shook as she strapped the belt around her waist. She clutched Milo as tightly as she could. The ship lurched and she heard a great rushing in her head.

They were on the move.